Whiskers
the Lonely
Kitten

Whiskers
the Lonely
Kitten

Holly Webb

Illustrated by Sophy Williams

SCHOLASTIC INC.

For everyone remembering a much-missed cat

ISBN 978-0-545-47436-8

12 11 10 9 8 7 6 5 4 3 2 1   12 13 14 15 16 17/0

Printed in the U.S.A.   40
First Scholastic printing, November 2012

Chapter One

"Oh, Mia, look! I told you Mrs. Johnston had a new cat. Isn't she adorable? So fluffy!" Mia's mom stroked the little black cat, who was sitting proudly on Mrs. Johnston's front wall.

Mia's best friend, Emily, tickled the purring cat under the chin. "She's so cute!"

Mia's mom looked over at Mia hopefully, then sighed. She hadn't even glanced up as Mom and Emily petted the cat. She was staring firmly at her shoes as she marched on down the road. It was as if she hadn't heard.

Mom and Emily exchanged worried looks and hurried after her. Emily lived a few doors down from Mia, and the girls usually walked to school together. Their moms and Mia's grandmother took turns going with them, now that Emily's big sister, Leah, had started middle school. Gran lived in a little apartment on the side of Mia's house, and took care of Mia when her parents were working. She'd moved in with them a few years ago, when she'd been ill and it had been difficult for her to live on her own.

"See you tomorrow, Mia!" Emily called as she turned into her driveway.

"Bye! Call me if you get stuck on that homework!" Mia was very good at math, and Emily wasn't. Emily had been moaning about their math homework all the way back from school.

Mia flung off her coat and hurried upstairs before Mom could start going on about Mrs. Johnston's adorable cat again. She could hear her mom asking her if she was okay, if she wanted a drink or to chat, but she ignored her.

Mia just didn't want to hear it. She'd never realized before how many cats there were in her neighborhood, or on the way to school. Now that she couldn't bear to see them, there seemed to be cats everywhere.

She slumped down on her bed and looked sadly at the navy blue fleece blanket spread over her comforter at the foot of the bed. It had a pattern of little cat faces scattered over it— and there were still orange cat hairs clinging onto it here and there. Sandy had slept on it every night for as long as Mia could remember. She still woke up in the middle of the night expecting her old cat to be there—sometimes she even reached down to pet him, waiting for his sleepy purr as he felt her move. It was so hard to believe that he was really gone.

She looked at the photo on her windowsill. It had been taken a couple months earlier, during summer vacation, just a few weeks before Sandy died. He was looking thin, and they'd taken him to the vet, but the day they took the photo he'd been enjoying the late summer sun in the yard. Mia had been sure he was getting better. Looking back now, she realized that he hadn't been jumping and pouncing and chasing the butterflies like he usually did, just lying quietly in the sun. But she hadn't wanted to believe that there was anything wrong with him.

Tears stung her eyes as she touched the glass over the photo, wishing she had the real Sandy snuggled up on her lap.

How could Mom keep pointing out other cats and expecting her to want to stop and pet them? Dad had even suggested going to the cat rescue center to look for a kitten! Mia didn't want a kitten, ever. She was never going to replace her beautiful Sandy.

Mom was calling her from downstairs, asking if she wanted a snack. Brushing the tears away, Mia carefully straightened Sandy's blanket and went down to the kitchen.

She could tell that Mom was watching her worriedly as she ate her apple. It only made her feel worse.

"I think I'll go and fill up the bird feeder," she said, wanting an excuse to leave the room. Mia knew Mom was only trying to help, but she really wasn't, and any minute now she was going to start talking about kittens again, or about getting a rabbit, like she'd suggested yesterday.

Mia grabbed the bag of bird seed from the cupboard and let herself out the back door, taking a deep breath of relief. A blackbird skittered out of her way as she went over to refill the feeder, and she murmured to it soothingly as she unhooked the wire case.

"It's all right, I'll be gone in a minute. And I'll probably drop some that you can come and peck up." She poured in the seed, and then hung up the feeder and perched on the arm of the bench, shivering a little in the autumn sun. She didn't want to go back inside just yet.

All of a sudden, a damp nose butted her hand, and Mia jumped, a strange, silly hope flooding into her.

But when she turned around, it wasn't her beautiful Sandy playing tricks on her. It was a pretty, plump white cat with blue eyes, and Mia recognized her. Silky, her friend Emily's cat.

"Hi, Silky," she whispered. "You look a little fat, kitty. Emily needs to stop giving you so many treats."

Silky rubbed up against her affectionately. Cats always liked Mia, and Silky already knew her, since Mia spent lots of time over at Emily's house. Sandy had known Emily, too, although he'd always chased Silky if she came into his yard.

This yard.

Mia swallowed and gently pushed Silky away, then walked quickly back into the house.

Her mom was standing by the kitchen window—she'd been watching, and she sighed, very quietly, as Mia hurried back inside.

"Are you okay, sweetheart?" she asked.

"I'm going to do my homework," Mia muttered, trying not to sound tearful. She was so sick of people worrying about her. Dad had talked to her for a long time at breakfast that morning about Sandy. But she was perfectly all right! Why couldn't everyone just leave her alone?

Chapter Two

Mia and her grandmother called to Emily on their way to school the next morning. Emily waved at them through the front window as they walked up, and then she disappeared and flung open the door.

"Guess what!" Emily shrieked.

Mia shook her head, laughing as Emily came running down the path. "What?

You finished the math homework and it was easy?"

Emily shuddered and made a face. "No, it was awful—I don't even want to think about it. I have to tell you—you'll never guess. We think Silky is going to have kittens!"

Gran smiled delightedly, and Mia gasped. "What, really? Kittens? When will she have them?"

"We're not quite sure. Mom's going to take her to the vet today to check. We were looking at her last night, and we just realized how big she'd gotten around the middle! Mom's a little annoyed, though. Well, she's excited, but she says it's going to be a big fuss, and we'll have to find homes for all the kittens." Emily frowned. "But Leah and I are going to work on Mom to let us keep one of them."

"Oh, wow . . ." Mia murmured. "You know, Silky came into our garden yesterday, and I thought she was looking plump. But I didn't realize she was having kittens!" *I didn't pay much attention to her before I pushed her*

away, Mia added in her head, feeling a little guilty.

Emily chattered on happily about the kittens all the way to school, wondering how many there would be, and whether they'd be white like Silky.

Mia joined in with a comment here and there, but thoughts were buzzing around inside her head. She still loved cats, of course she did. But it was definitely hard to be around them right now, when every cat seemed to remind her so much of Sandy. It wouldn't be as difficult if her mom and dad weren't so interested in getting another pet—they seemed to think Mia needed another cat to be able to get over Sandy. And now Emily was all excited about kittens, too.

"What's the matter, Mia? You've gotten so quiet," Emily asked as they waved to Gran and went into the school.

Mia smiled and shook her head. "I'm fine. I'm glad I'm walking home with you and my mom today—can we stop in and see Silky, and ask your mom what the vet said?" She was trying hard to sound excited, like she knew she should, and it must have worked, because Emily beamed at her.

"Of course you can!" Emily said, giving her a hug. "I can't wait to tell everyone about Silky having kittens! I just hope it's true!"

19

Emily told Mia's mom the news as soon as they came out of school. She'd come straight from work to pick them up and hadn't spoken to Gran, so it was a total surprise.

"Oh, Mia, isn't that great? Kittens!"

"Mmm." Mia tried to sound enthusiastic. She really didn't want to spoil things for Emily. "Can we go and see Silky on the way home?" she asked. "Emily's mom took Silky to the vet, so she should know for certain by now—maybe she'll even know when the kittens might be born."

Mom nodded. "Of course!"

They hurried back to Emily's house, and Emily burst through the door, racing ahead and calling for her mom. "What did the vet say? Is she definitely having kittens? When will they come?"

"Sooner than we thought!" her mom said, laughing. "Could be only a couple of weeks, the vet said. And she felt Silky's tummy, and she thinks there are at least three kittens, possibly more."

"Three!" Emily breathed, crouching down next to Silky, who was curled up in her furry basket. "That explains why she's so fat!"

Mia sat down next to her friend and petted Silky gently. She was very well-named—her fur was beautifully soft and smooth. She wasn't asleep, but her pretty blue eyes were half-closed, as though she was tired. She probably was, Mia thought.

"Three kittens to find homes for." Her mom sighed. She looked thoughtfully at Mia's mom. "I don't suppose . . ."

Mia saw her mom smile and glance over at her, raising her eyebrows. Emily's mom glanced at her, too, and nodded understandingly. Mia could tell exactly what Mom meant—*Maybe, but I'm not sure about Mia.*

She gave Silky one last gentle pet. It was odd to think that there were tiny kittens squirming around inside her.

"Mom, I've got tons of homework," she pointed out, getting to her feet. "We'd better go." They didn't really need to leave that minute, but she didn't want her mom and Emily's mom exchanging any more of those secret looks.

The subject didn't go away, though. Dad was full of questions at dinnertime, wanting to know when the kittens would arrive, and what Silky had looked like.

"Silky's such a sweet cat," he said, looking at Mia. "She'll have cute kittens, Mia, don't you think?"

Mia nodded. "But they won't be as beautiful as Sandy," she said, eyeing her dad firmly. "We'll never find another cat like him."

He shook his head with a sigh. "No, I suppose not. But different can be good, too, you know, Mia."

When she went up to bed that night, Mia lay there for a long time, hugging Sandy's blanket and thinking. She'd never actually had a kitten of her own. Sandy had been older than she was—he was about two when she was born. Gran had a nice photo of him that she kept in her little living room, one that Mom and Dad had sent her when she still lived in her old house, before she came to live with them all a few years later. It was a photo of Mia as a baby, sitting up in her bouncy chair and reaching out a fat little hand for Sandy's tail as he strolled past.

Mom had photos of Sandy as a kitten, too, in her photo album.

He'd been super cute—with round green eyes that looked too big for his little whiskery face, and apricot-pink pads on his paws. They were darker by the time Mia knew him, from going outside and roughening them up. But he was still beautiful, and his eyes were like emeralds.

Mia gulped and buried her face in the blanket. It still smelled like him. She really wanted to be excited for Emily, but even the thought of kittens made her miss Sandy so much. She wasn't sure she could bear to see them for real.

Chapter Three

"I wonder if there's any news yet!" Emily said excitedly as they put on their coats at the end of school. "Mom's picking us up today—I can't wait to ask her. Silky's been a little shy and weird all weekend, then she went off and snuggled herself up in the hall cupboard this morning. I'm sure that means she's 'nesting,' getting ready for her kittens to come."

It was Monday, two weeks since Emily had found out Silky was having kittens, and she had been getting more and more impatient every day.

Mia smiled. Even though the thought of kittens made her miss Sandy, she could see how happy Emily was. They hurried outside, looking eagerly for Emily's mom. But she wasn't there—instead, Mia's grandmother was waving at them from by the gate.

"Gran! What are you doing here?" Mia called in surprise.

Gran smiled. "Silky's having her kittens! Your mom didn't want to leave her on her own, Emily, so she called me. My legs aren't too bad today, so I was glad to come out for a walk."

"She's having them right now?" Emily squealed in delight, whirling her schoolbag around. "Ooooh, how many are there?"

"Four so far, apparently, and your mom thought that might be it, but she wasn't quite sure."

"Four kittens!" Emily said blissfully, and even Mia felt her stomach squirm with excitement. "Can Mia come in and see them, Mrs. Lovett?" Emily asked Mia's grandmother.

"I don't think so today," Gran said thoughtfully. "They were just born, and Silky will be tired and very protective of her new babies. She won't want a lot of visitors. You can tell Mia about them tomorrow."

Emily walked home so fast she was practically running, and she dashed into her house with a wave, leaving Mia and Gran to walk on to their house.

"You're looking serious, Mia," Gran commented. "Aren't you excited about the kittens?"

Mia was silent for a moment. The walk home and Emily's happy chattering about Silky's babies had brought back that strange, miserable feeling again, even worse than before. It seemed so unfair that Emily should have her beautiful Silky and four cute little kittens, too. She wasn't jealous of Emily, exactly—just sad.

"I was," she admitted. "When you told us they were coming, I thought it was wonderful. But then Emily started talking about how sweet they'd be, and how she was looking forward to cuddling them and playing with them. And it just made me miss Sandy so much!" She leaned her face against Gran's arm. "I'm not even sure I want to go and see them," she whispered.

Gran nodded thoughtfully. "I wondered if that was it. Poor Mia." She gave her a hug as they reached their driveway. "Come on, let's go make some hot chocolate Perhaps that will cheer you up a little."

Emily was full of news of the kittens the next day at school. Their friends Libby and Poppy rushed up to her, desperate to know what had happened. Mia did her best to join in and sound enthusiastic, but it was hard.

"There's a black one, and two tabbies, and the last one to be born was a tiny, tiny little white one, with the most enormous set of whiskers!" Emily beamed at Mia. "Do you think you can come and see them after school?"

Mia hesitated. She could—but she was worried she'd do something awful like start crying. "Um, I'm not sure," she said slowly. "Gran's picking me up, and she said something about going shopping."

"Oh." Emily looked a bit surprised, as though she'd been expecting Mia to be more excited, and Mia felt guilty.

"Did you learn those spelling words?" she asked quickly, to try and distract Emily from the kittens.

Emily made a face. "Well, I looked at them. . . . But then the kittens were so fun to watch—they're all just nosing around each other and Silky and squeaking, and it's so funny. I probably haven't learned the words very well." She sighed. "Can you test me?"

Mia nodded, feeling relieved. She'd gotten away with it for today, but she wasn't going to be able to keep on making excuses. Sooner or later, she was going to have to go and see the kittens.

By the end of the week, Mia had run out of excuses to give Emily, and Emily was running out of patience. On Friday at lunchtime, she told Mia that her mom said she could come over that weekend to see the kittens if she wanted.

Mia's mind went blank. What could she possibly say, except that she didn't want to? She couldn't pretend to be busy for the whole weekend.

"So will you come?" Emily asked, staring at her and frowning slightly.

Mia opened her mouth, and then closed it again helplessly.

"You don't want to, do you?" Emily said. Her voice was flat, and Mia could see that she was really hurt. It made Mia feel terrible.

"Sorry . . ." she whispered.

"Is it because of Sandy?" Emily asked. She sounded like she was trying to be angry, but she couldn't quite get there. Emily could never argue. When she and Mia had a fight, it usually only lasted two minutes before Emily cried.

Mia nodded. "It's not that I don't want you to have them—I just miss Sandy, and you having all those kittens . . ."

"I know you miss Sandy," Emily said, her voice getting sniffly already.

"But you're supposed to be my best friend, and you should at least try to be happy for me! I really wanted to show them to you."

Mia nodded. She felt like she might cry now, too. "I know! I really am trying! I just can't make myself stop being sad about him. I can't be happy about the kittens. I can't do it!"

Emily stared back at her, tears welling up in her brown eyes, and then she gave a huge sniff and ran off to hide in the corner of the playground behind one of the benches.

Mia stared after her sadly. She knew she should go after her friend, say sorry, and promise that of course she'd go and see the kittens. But her feet just wouldn't move.

It was a very strange walk home. Mia and Emily didn't talk to each other, and Mia's grandmother, who'd come to pick them up, could hardly get them to talk to her, either. For Mia, it was a relief when Emily ducked through her front door.

"What on earth's the matter?" Gran asked as they took off their coats in the hallway. "Have you two had an argument?"

"Sort of," Mia admitted.

"Well, I hope you're going to make up, Mia. You both looked so miserable. Can't you talk to her about it? Why don't you give her a call?"

Mia shook her head. "It wasn't really that sort of fight. We didn't shout at each other or anything. It's mostly my fault, and Emily won't be my friend unless I can make it up to her. But I can't." She sniffed. She'd spent the whole afternoon feeling awful, and now that she was at home with only Gran to see, she felt like just letting herself cry.

Gran hugged her. "Oh, Mia. Why

don't you tell me? Maybe talking to someone else will help."

Mia shook her head. "I don't think it will," she whispered. But she let Gran lead her into her little living room, and sat down on the sofa with her.

Gran gave her a tissue. "Go on, Mia. What happened?"

"She wants me to go and see her kittens."

"And you can't?"

Mia leaned against her shoulder. "It makes me too sad," she murmured. "Mom and Dad keep talking about us getting another pet—a rabbit, or even another cat. It's like everyone has forgotten Sandy."

Gran sighed. "I don't think that's true, Mia. Your mom and dad are just trying to cheer you up. We all loved Sandy—you know that. Though I do understand he was your special cat."

"I really, really miss him," Mia said tearfully. "Mom and Dad won't listen to me. They think I should have gotten over it by now, and I'm just being silly!"

"Oh, Mia, they really don't think that. They just want you to be happy."

"But it was August when he died, and it's only October now. I haven't stopped missing him yet." Mia sniffed. "I can't imagine *not* missing him! And now I can't even say anything about it to Emily, because she's so excited about her kittens. I tried to explain, but she didn't understand."

"It's such a special time for her,"

Gran said, stroking Mia's hair. "She can't help being happy about it, can she?"

"I guess not. I just wish I could be happy along with her, that's all."

"Are you sure you want to be happy?" Gran said thoughtfully, and Mia sat up and stared at her.

"Of course I am! I don't *want* to be miserable!"

"But I think you're hanging on to being sad, Mia. If you're miserable, someone's still missing Sandy and it's as if he's still here. Do you see what I mean?"

Mia shook her head. "It isn't like that. . . ." But her voice trailed off. Maybe it was, a little bit.

"Look." Gran got up and fetched a little photo album from a shelf.

"I've been making this for you, Mia, but I wasn't going to give it to you yet, in case it just made you more upset."

"Oh, Gran! All these photos of Sandy . . ." Mia turned the pages, laughing as Sandy turned from a little orange fluffball into the big, handsome cat she remembered. "He was so special," she said sadly.

"Do you know what I noticed most of all about these photos?" Gran asked, smiling at a photo from Christmas, of Sandy lying in a pile of wrapping paper, a ribbon wrapped around his paws. "He was always such a happy cat."

Mia smiled. It was true.

"Except those last couple of weeks, when he was sick. He was so tired—he wasn't really himself anymore. He'd purr if we petted him, especially for you. But most of the time, he just slept."

Mia nodded. "He didn't even want to eat."

"Exactly. And Sandy loved his food!"

Mia giggled. Mom was always getting annoyed with Sandy, beacuse if she left anything lying around in the kitchen while she was cooking and she turned her back for a second, a sneaky orange paw would swipe it. He even ate mushrooms, which was very unusual for a cat.

"He wasn't happy at the end, was he?" she murmured.

Gran shook her head. "No. And he loved you so much, Mia. He hated it when you were sad about something, didn't he?"

"Like that time I fell over." Mia closed her eyes, remembering. She'd fallen down the stairs and banged her arm— she hadn't actually broken it, but it had still really hurt. She'd been moping around the house with it all bandaged up until Sandy had come over to her while she was lying on the sofa. He sat on her chest and stared at her, dangling his big white whiskers in her face and purring like a lawn mower. It was as though he was determined to cheer her up. And of course it worked!

"You're right." She turned to the last picture in the album. It showed her and Emily, both holding Sandy—he was big enough for two girls to hold. They were both grinning at the camera, and Sandy looked so pleased with himself.

"Emily's your best friend, Mia. You have to make an effort for friends, even if it's hard sometimes."

Mia nodded. "I know. I'll call Emily and say I'm sorry, and I'll go and see the kittens soon. Maybe on Monday. And I'll try to stop missing Sandy so much, Gran. I really will."

Chapter Four

Gran must have told Mom about the talk she'd had with Mia, because on Monday morning Mom said she'd walk Mia to school, and they'd stop and pick up Emily on the way.

"Maybe you can pop in and see the kittens this morning," Mom suggested. "Not for long, though, because you and Emily can't be late for school. Okay?"

Mia nodded and gave her mom a quick hug. She could see what Mom was doing. She was giving Mia a chance to see the kittens for just a couple of minutes. If it made her too sad, they could say they had to get to school.

Emily and her mom were waiting for them at the door. Mom had probably texted Emily's mom about it, Mia thought. She felt a sudden rush of love for Mom and Gran, worrying about her and trying to make everything okay again. Their worrying had gotten on her nerves before, but they were only being nice.

"Come and see, come and see!" Emily grabbed her. "When we came down this morning, they'd opened their eyes. They're so cute!" She stopped pulling Mia along and looked at her worriedly.

"You still want to see them, don't you?"

Mia nodded. "Of course. And I'm sorry I've been such a grump."

"Oh, you weren't!" Emily hugged her.

Mia was still anxious as she followed Emily into the warm kitchen. Silky and the kittens had a little pen that Emily's mom had made out of pieces of an old bookcase. It was close to the radiator to make sure the kittens stayed warm.

"Just look at them," Emily said proudly. "Aren't they the most beautiful things you've ever seen?"

Mia glanced in the pen, and Silky yawned hugely and stared back at her. She looked as though she agreed with Emily entirely, and she expected Mia to agree, too. There was a definite look of pride on her pretty white face as she gazed down at her new family.

The kittens were wriggling around next to their mom. Just as Mia leaned closer, the black kitten, who seemed to be the biggest (although it was hard to tell), climbed right on top of the tiny white one, who gave an indignant squeak.

"Oh, no! Is he okay?" Mia asked anxiously, but Emily only giggled.

"I'm sure he is. They do that all the time! I wondered if it would get better when they opened their eyes, but they still just walk all over one another. And they're so greedy and pushy about getting to Silky for their milk."

"He's the boy, isn't he? The little white one?" Emily had told Mia that they'd figured out that there were three girls and one boy.

Emily nodded. "He's cute, isn't he?"

"They all are." Mia crouched down by the pen, glancing at Silky first to make sure she wasn't bothered by it. But the white cat looked like she was enjoying showing off her babies. The two tabby kittens were suckling, and the black one was trying to reach Silky's side, too. But the little white kitten stayed curled up near his mom's front paws. He yawned, and then gazed up at Mia with dark, dark blue eyes.

Mia knew that he was so small he probably couldn't see her very well, but somehow he seemed to be looking right at her, and he wrinkled his nose and made a tiny little mew.

Mia smiled and reached out her fingers for the kitten to sniff. How could she have thought anything so adorable would make her sad?

After that, Mia found that the thought of the kittens didn't upset her anymore. Maybe it was because none of them were orange, like her Sandy. They were themselves instead, and although she still missed Sandy, the kittens were so cute that they mostly just made her laugh. Especially the white kitten, who seemed so loving. He always nuzzled at her and licked her fingers.

One Friday afternoon, a couple of weeks after the kittens were born, Mia went over to play at Emily's house. She was really looking forward to it. She'd stopped in to see the kittens quite a few times since her first visit, but had never stayed long. Somehow there hadn't been a chance to spend very much time with the kittens.

Mia followed Emily into the kitchen. It had been two or three days since she'd last seen the kittens, and she gasped as she got closer to their pen.

"They're so much bigger!"

Emily laughed. "I know! It's amazing, isn't it?"

Mia shook her head. "It's like someone's blown them up, like little furry balloons." She crouched down to look more closely at the four kittens in their pen. One of the tabbies was stomping determinedly across the soft blankets on the floor, while the other three kittens were feeding. "They look more cat-shaped, somehow. Do you know what I mean? They were just tiny fluffy balls before, but now they're mini-cats. Oh, look!"

The white kitten seemed to have heard her talking. He stopped feeding and looked around curiously, trying to figure out where her voice was coming from. Then he stumbled toward her, uttering that tiny squeak of a meow she'd heard before.

"Hello, sweetie," Mia whispered, and the kitten meowed back, trying to scrabble his way up the side of the pen.

"Wow! He's never done that before!" Emily murmured, her eyes wide.

"Can I hold him?" Mia asked hopefully. "Would Silky mind?"

Silky was still feeding one of the tabbies and the black kitten, but she had her head up, and she was watching Mia and the white kitten carefully.

"It should be okay, don't you think, Mom?" Emily asked. "We've picked them up before, and you can tell he wants you to!"

Very gently, Mia reached into the pen and scooped up the white kitten, snuggling him carefully in her lap.

The kitten let out a little breath of a purr, padding at her skirt with his paws. Then he curled up with a contented sigh. This was what he had wanted.

"He's so soft!" Mia whispered. "And I'm sure his whiskers have grown since I last saw him. Just look at them!"

The kitten stared up at her. He liked her voice. He recognized it from when she had come before, and the girl's smell. She had petted him, and he'd wanted her to cuddle him. He yawned and his waterfall of white whiskers shimmered.

"None of the others have whiskers like that!" Mia laughed. "You should call him Whiskers, Emily. You haven't named them yet, have you?"

Emily shook her head. She had a huge smile suddenly. "Well, we've only named the black kitten, because we're keeping her! She's going to be my birthday present!" She picked up the black kitten, who seemed to have fallen asleep while she was feeding. "I'm calling her Satin, to go with Silky—get it?" She snuggled the kitten under her chin lovingly.

"You're so lucky!" Mia smiled, but her stomach turned over. Of course. The kittens would have to go to new owners. She sighed, and the white kitten made a little grumbling noise as the comfy lap he was on shifted. She'd only known Whiskers—she couldn't help calling him that, even though she knew it wouldn't be his real name—for a couple of weeks, but already she knew she would miss him.

Chapter Five

Whiskers wriggled himself farther into the cozy fold of the blanket. He was still very tiny, but he was starting to understand more about the world, and today the world felt *cold*. He didn't like it. Usually he would have snuggled up next to his mother, but she had disappeared. Now that he and his sisters were a little bigger—nearly four weeks old—she did that every so often.

Something soft landed in the pen next to him, and Whiskers twitched and woke out of his half-doze. It was a big, round, bright thing. He had no idea what it was. Neither did his two tabby sisters, who prowled toward it together, hissing fiercely. They were very good at being fierce. Whiskers and Satin watched worriedly as one of the tabby kittens dabbed a paw at the pink thing. It bounced a little. She tapped it again, and it wobbled in an interesting way, so she jabbed at it again, with her claws out this time.

The balloon burst with an enormous *bang*, and the tabby kittens jumped back in surprise, eyeing the shriveled bit of pink rubber that was left. Whiskers cowered back in the corner of the pen, meowing with fright and wishing his mother would come back. He had no idea what had happened! How had the round pink thing disappeared, and why had there been that terrible noise?

Silky shot back into the room, convinced that someone was hurting her babies, and leaped into the pen, checking them all frantically. Whiskers pressed up against her, shivering.

"I'm sorry, kittens." Emily crouched down by the pen. "I didn't mean to scare you. It was only a balloon—I'm blowing them up for my birthday party, and that one must have rolled off the table."

Whiskers meowed again, eyeing the other strange large, round things he could see on the kitchen table. Did that mean there were going to be more horrible noises? When Emily tried to give him a comforting pet he let her, but he was trembling, and showing his tiny little teeth.

"Oh, no," Emily said sadly. "It really scared you, didn't it? I'm sorry. But I've got some good news. Mia's coming later, and she's staying the night. That'll be nice, won't it? You love Mia, don't you?" She sighed to herself, almost angrily. "And Mia loves you, too—she just doesn't know it yet."

Mia had been visiting the kittens almost every day, and she always went straight for Whiskers. "I wish she'd just hurry up and figure out that she should take you home," Emily told Whiskers sadly. "Mom's already talking about looking for new homes for you in a few weeks. I've given Mia tons of hints, but she doesn't get them at all, and I don't want to come out and say it in case it makes her upset about Sandy again."

She tickled Whiskers behind the ears. "You want to be Mia's kitten, don't you, Whiskers? You never play as nicely with anyone else. And you're always sad when she goes home. You meowed after her yesterday, and you looked really lonely, even though you were cuddled up next to Silky." She sighed. "Anyway, you'll all have to be super-cute tonight for my sleepover," she told the kittens, half-seriously. "Mia's coming, and Libby and Poppy. At least, they are if it doesn't snow before then. It's so cold now! You'd better groom your babies, Silky. Put their party fur on!"

"Oh, did you do all the balloons, Emily? Good. I'll hang them up in the hall—you go and get changed. Leah's just putting the birthday banner on the front door." Emily's mom hurried into the kitchen and gave her a quick hug. "Are you excited about your party?"

Emily nodded, laughing. "Of course I am. But it's so chilly! I'm not sure about sleeping on the living-room floor now!"

Her mom nodded. "I know, I hope

it doesn't get too much colder before Christmas. It's still only November."

Leah came in, rubbing her fingers. "I'm frozen," she moaned, but then her eyes widened. "Hey, look at Satin!"

The black kitten was teetering on the edge of the pen, and as they watched, she half-jumped, half-fell onto the kitchen floor, where she stood up and shook herself, trying to look as though she meant to do exactly that.

"Oh, my goodness . . ." Mom muttered. "We're in for it now. They'll be everywhere. We'll have to remember to keep the kitchen door closed. Of course they would choose today of all days to start getting out!"

The two tabby kittens were now standing on their back legs, peering over the top of the pen and staring at their sister with huge round eyes, as if they couldn't believe what she'd managed to do. Satin had set off to investigate the kitchen and was sniffing thoughtfully around the table legs.

"Shall I let her explore for a while?" Emily asked, and Mom nodded.

"I expect she'll wear herself out soon. Go and get changed—they'll all be here any minute! Just make sure you shut the kitchen door!"

Mia looked at the kittens a little

anxiously. Libby and Poppy had just arrived, and the kitchen had suddenly gotten very noisy. She hoped Silky and the kittens wouldn't mind.

But Satin and the two tabby kittens were loving the attention. They put on a beautiful performance of stalking a piece of yarn, and then climbed all over Libby and Poppy. Satin then snuggled up on Libby's knee, while the tabbies fought each other for the wool. Only Whiskers was still in the kitten pen, hiding behind Silky.

"The little white kitten's so cute!" Poppy said, reaching into the pen to pick him up. Whiskers shied away from her, but she didn't seem to notice—she grabbed him and took him out of his nice, safe pen, dangling

him in front of her.

"Don't scare him!" Mia said worriedly. She was itching to snatch Whiskers away from Poppy. It wasn't that Poppy meant to frighten him—she just didn't know how to hold him correctly. But Whiskers wasn't hers. She couldn't boss Poppy around. And if Mia grabbed him, he'd only be even more scared. Emily was out of the room, helping her mom put everyone's coats away, or Mia knew she'd have said something.

Poppy sat down on the floor, placing Whiskers on her lap and petting him. But he was upset now, and he hissed and dug in his claws as he scrambled to get away from the loud, scary girl.

Poppy squeaked. "Ow, he scratched me!" She jerked her leg, and Whiskers slipped off her lap, landing on the floor with a worried meow.

"Sshh, sshh . . . Come here, Whiskers." Mia stretched out a hand to him gently, and he gladly crept over to her, burrowing into her skirt as she put him on her lap.

"He didn't mean to scratch you," she told Poppy. "He's just a little shyer than the other kittens."

Poppy nodded. "He's sweet, but I like the tabby ones more. They're so cute and active! Oh, look, that one's got yarn all wrapped around her paws!"

Mia petted Whiskers and sighed. He was cute, too, like when his huge whiskers wobbled when he yawned, and how he always put his front paws in the food bowl, now that the kittens were starting to eat solid food. It was just that since Satin and the tabbies were so much bouncier, everyone always noticed them first.

"You need to be a little more friendly," she whispered to Whiskers. "You won't find an owner if you keep hiding in your pen. A few weeks from now, people will be coming to see if they want to take you home. You've got to show everybody how adorable you are." She smiled, somewhat sadly. She wanted Whiskers to have a nice home of his own, but if he stayed at Emily's, it meant she'd be able to keep on seeing him. Emily's mom kept saying they were only keeping Satin, but if they couldn't find a nice owner for Whiskers, she might change her mind, right?

Whiskers didn't know what Mia was saying, but he liked listening to her, and she made him feel safe. He purred, very quietly, and nuzzled her hand.

"Should we watch the movie in our sleeping bags?" Emily suggested as she took a bag of popcorn out of the microwave. "Oh, this smells delicious."

"Definitely sleeping bags," Poppy agreed.

"Can we bring the kittens?" Libby asked hopefully.

Emily's mom looked thoughtful. "I suppose for a little while. But they'll probably want to be back with Silky soon. And after the movie, girls, you need to go to sleep! It's getting late."

The girls all nodded angelically, but Emily winked at Mia behind her mom's back. "I've got a secret chocolate supply," she whispered. "Are you bringing Whiskers?"

Mia nodded. "If you think he won't mind. He likes staying in the pen, doesn't he?"

Emily shook her head. "Not if it's you cuddling him."

Mia blushed. "Do you think he likes me that much?"

Emily rolled her eyes. "Of course he does! Come on!"

Mia went into the living room and snuggled up in her sleeping bag—even with the heat on high, it was still chilly. Emily's mom had said they'd better all sleep in a huddle to keep warm, like penguins, and she'd found lots of extra blankets. Whiskers sat on Mia's tummy, purring quietly to himself. He was happy. He hadn't been sure about the loud girls, or people grabbing him, but now he had Mia, and she didn't seem to be going anywhere, like she usually was. He could even put up with the noisy girls if Mia was there, too.

Mia hardly paid attention to the movie at all. She was watching Whiskers, snuggled up on her sleeping bag, and petting him gently. His fur was so soft—and he was such a little cat, so different from Sandy.

As the movie went on, the other kittens padded back to the kitchen, looking for Silky and their pen. But Whiskers curled up on top of Mia and fell fast asleep—and he was still there the next morning.

Chapter Six

"Oh, Mia!" Dad laughed. "How did you get him to do that?" He'd just arrived to pick up Mia from the sleepover. Libby and Poppy had already left—they had to hurry off to a dance class.

Mia shook her head very, very carefully. "I didn't, Dad. He just climbed up there. I think he's eyeing my toast."

From his place on her shoulder, Whiskers purred loudly, and Mia giggled as his long whiskers tickled her cheek. "I wish I didn't have to go home and say good-bye to you!"

Her dad exchanged a thoughtful glance with Emily's mom. "When will the kittens be ready to go to new homes?"

"Well, I was looking it up, and it seems that about ten or twelve weeks old would be best. Ours are four weeks now, so they'll be ten weeks old about halfway through December. So I thought around then. It's a little close to Christmas, which is the only problem. Everyone's so busy, and I don't want to be encouraging people to give kittens as presents."

"Why not?" Mia asked. She thought a kitten would be a lovely Christmas present. Emily was getting Satin for her birthday, after all.

"Well, people sometimes get a kitten for their children for Christmas, but don't really think about them growing up into big cats who need to be taken care of. Then sometimes they're abandoned," Emily's mom added sadly. "Luckily, most kittens are born in the spring or summertime. Silky was a little late!"

Mia reached up and tickled Whiskers under the chin. She could feel his purrs buzzing against her neck.

I could take you home, she thought to herself, just for a second. But then she remembered. She didn't want another cat—not after Sandy. Very gently, she reached up, lifted Whiskers off her shoulder, and took him over to the pen. "Sorry, sweetie, I have to go."

Whiskers stared at her in surprise. Had Mia not liked him sitting on her shoulder? Why was she going? He wailed—a loud, sad kitten wail that made Mia flinch as she scuttled into the hallway to grab her stuff.

She said good-bye to Emily quickly. She felt bad, rushing off, but she just couldn't stay any longer. She was almost silent on the walk home, even though Dad kept trying to ask about the party.

"Mia, have you thought . . . ?" Dad started as they carried her things into the house. "Emily's mom talking about homes for the kittens made me wonder. You seem to get along with Whiskers so well. . . ."

He trailed off when Mia looked up at him with her eyes full of tears.

"I can't," she whispered. "I thought I could, but what about Sandy? I'm not going to forget him! I never, ever want another cat again!"

"You don't have to forget him, Mia. . . ." Dad tried to say, but Mia raced off upstairs to her room and slammed the door behind her.

Over the next few weeks, Emily kept Mia updated as they started to look for new homes for the kittens. Her mom had put an ad in the newspaper, and up in local shops that had message boards. A couple of people had called about coming to see them already.

"Someone named Maria is coming over on Saturday to see them all," she told Mia as they ate their packed lunches. "I'm sort of half-excited, half-sad. I really want them all to have nice homes." Emily shook her head. "And at least we're keeping Satin."

Mia nodded. She wanted them to have good homes, too. Especially Whiskers. He needed a home with someone who could love him completely, without always remembering another cat. It was no use for Emily and Mom and Dad to give her all those hopeful looks. Sandy was her forever cat. She couldn't replace him, not even with Whiskers.

Emily's mom showed Maria into the kitchen, where Emily and Leah were playing with the kittens.

"Oh, aren't they sweet! How many are there?" Maria asked, laughing as one of the tabbies sniffed her boots.

"Four, but we're keeping Satin—the black kitten. There are two female tabbies, and the little white boy. Did you want just one kitten?" Emily's mom asked. "We're thinking that the tabby girls might want to stay together —they're such a team."

"I was only planning on getting one," Maria said. "I can't see a white kitten. . . ."

"He was here a minute ago!" Leah looked around the kitchen. "Now that they can climb out of their pen they're all over the place."

"He's a little shy," Emily's mom explained. "But he's very sweet once he gets used to you. Look, there he is!" She smiled and pointed to the pen, where a little white head was poking out under the fleecy blanket. "I'll get him out." She picked Whiskers up and tried to pass him to Maria, but he squeaked in fright and then hissed, his paws sticking out rigidly, and his tail fluffed out to twice its usual size.

"Oh, dear—don't make him if he doesn't want to," Maria said worriedly. "Poor thing, he really is nervous. There are a lot of cats around where I live, and I'm not sure this little one would cope very well if he's so shy. I'm sorry— I'm sure you'll find wonderful homes for them all."

Emily's mom followed her to the door, and Emily and Leah looked down at Whiskers, who was now huddled in Leah's arms.

"Oh, Whiskers," Emily muttered. "No one's going to want you if you do that every time. It's so stupid! He wants to be Mia's kitten, I know he does."

Leah nodded. "I know. But we can't force her to take him. Maybe she'll come around to the idea."

Emily sighed. "I wish she'd hurry up about it."

A couple of weeks later, Mia and her grandmother stopped in on the way home from school, and found that only Whiskers and Satin were left.

"I'm not surprised Whiskers didn't like them. The two little boys were very noisy," Emily's mom was saying to Gran. "They thought Whiskers was beautiful, and they were ready to choose him, but it was just like with Maria. They tried to cuddle him, and he actually shot out the kitchen door and went and hid in the cupboard! So they decided they'd take the tabbies instead." She laughed. "And they're going to name them Molly and Polly. I don't think they'll ever be able to remember which is which!"

"So it's only Whiskers now?" Mia asked as Emily's mom made Gran coffee. Mia sat petting the little ball of white fur curled up in her lap.

Emily nodded. "At least he's still got Satin to play with. But Mom's determined that we're only keeping one. We have to find Whiskers a home, and no one wants an unfriendly kitten."

"He isn't!" Mia said indignantly. "He's a sweetheart. He's just shy." *But maybe that's a good thing,* she admitted to herself. *I really don't want him to go. . . .*

Whiskers yawned and wriggled himself to be comfortable again. Mia and Emily had been rolling balls of newspaper for him and Satin to chase, and he was exhausted. The kitchen was covered in shredded paper, though. Whiskers and Satin had done a thorough job. He rolled over onto his back, all four paws in the air, showing off his fat pinkish tummy.

He was liking solid food more and more now, and after he'd had a meal, he looked like a little ball.

"But he's so different with you. . . ." Emily sighed. "He doesn't mind playing with me and Leah, and he'll let us pet him. But I don't think he's ever gone to sleep on me. And definitely not upside down! That means he really trusts you, you know."

Mia nodded. She didn't dare say anything, but she looked up at Gran. She was smiling, and nodding as if she agreed with Emily. Maybe Mia was being silly. Was it like Gran had said when the kittens were born, that she was still holding on to missing Sandy? Was she making herself sad on purpose? Maybe it was finally time to let Sandy go.

Chapter Seven

"I'll come and get you later, then, Mia," Gran said, one day after school. Gran gave her a kiss, and Mia waved good-bye. Whiskers was already weaving himself happily around her ankles, purring. His purr had definitely gotten louder as he got bigger, Mia decided. He was twelve weeks old now, certainly old enough for a new home.

But no one seemed to want a shy, nervous little white cat. Mia didn't mind. She was looking forward to spending lots of time with Whiskers over winter break. It had even started to snow that morning, although the flakes hadn't stuck. She was sure that Whiskers would look adorable if they took him out to play in the snow. He would be invisible, except for his round blue eyes!

Whiskers batted at her leg with his paw, asking to be picked up. Mia came to see him almost every day now, but he still missed her when she wasn't there. He wondered if one day she would take him with her.

"Hello, Mister Whiskers." Mia picked him up and cuddled him.

"What should we do today?"

"Homework!" Emily said, grinning and waving the sheet that Mrs. Jones, their teacher, had given them for the project they had to do over break. It was the last week of the term and neither of the girls really felt like working, but Mrs. Jones was known as the scariest teacher at their school. They needed to plan their project, even if it was only a little over a week till Christmas Day. "We have to figure out this project, remember? Come on, bring Whiskers with you." She scooped up Satin, leaving Silky alone in the hallway, looking quite relieved. Whiskers and Satin were so much bigger now, and so bouncy that they wore Silky out.

"I can smell fishsticks," Mia said, a while later. "So can Whiskers and Satin, look  at them!" The kittens were prowling up and down by Emily's bedroom door, their tails twitching eagerly.

"I think our plan sounds really good," Emily said, looking down at what they'd written. "*Animals in the time of Queen Victoria.* I bet no one else will have thought of that. It's a great idea, Mia."

Mia laughed. "I'll have the ideas, you do the writing. You almost finished the whole plan while I was just cuddling Whiskers. Do you think dinner's ready?

The smell of those fishsticks is making me hungry, too."

"Must be. Let's go and see." Emily opened the door, and the kittens shot out onto the landing and eyed the stairs uncertainly. They wanted to be down there with the delicious fishy smell— but they weren't really sure about stairs yet.

Whiskers looked at Mia pleadingly, and she laughed and picked him up. She carried him down to the kitchen, while Emily followed with Satin.

Emily's mom smiled as they came in. "Look at those kittens! I've never seen them look so hungry. We'd better find the fish-flavored kitten food."

"I think they'd rather just have the fishsticks," Emily said, going to the cupboard for the can, and spooning out the kitten food. "Ugh, this one smells the worst!"

But Satin and Whiskers raced for their bowls and gulped down the food eagerly.

Emily's mom had just passed Leah, Emily, and Mia their dinner when the phone rang. She went to answer it, fighting with her oven mitts. "Hello? Oh, yes . . . That's right. There's actually only one kitten left now."

Mia smiled, pausing with her fork halfway to her mouth. A paw was batting at her knee. Whiskers must have wolfed down his kitten food already, and now he was on the hunt for something even better. She scooped him up onto her lap and fed him a tiny bit of

fishstick. Emily's mom wasn't looking—
she was concentrating on the phone call.

"Oh, you've been looking for a white
kitten? That's wonderful. He is a little
bit shy, though, that's the only thing.
He's very friendly once he knows you,
but he may not want to be picked up."

The person on the other end of
the phone didn't seem to mind this.
Emily's mom was nodding and smiling.

Whiskers stared up at Mia, hoping
for some more fishstick. His whiskers
shook with excitement as he reached
up a little white paw to pat Mia's hand.

But she didn't give him any. She put
down her fork, very slowly and quietly,
and stared at him. The kitten's whiskers
drooped. Mia's face had changed. She
didn't look like the girl who'd been

sneaking him scraps a moment before. She was pale and miserable. Whiskers meowed, his ears flattening against his head. What was wrong?

"Tomorrow evening? Yes, that would be great. See you then." Emily's mom put down the phone, smiling. "Someone wants to come and see Whiskers! Her name's Miriam, and she says she's adopted a nervous cat before, so she doesn't mind if he's shy. And she's always wanted to have a white kitten. It's perfect!"

Emily nodded, but she was looking worriedly at Mia.

Mia gulped. It was. Whiskers was going to have a perfect home—and it wasn't with her. She'd let this happen. If only she'd been brave enough to say

that she wanted him to be her kitten
—that she still loved Sandy, but she'd
said good-bye to him.

She stood up jerkily,
huddling Whiskers
against her tummy,
and passed him to
Emily. "I'm sorry,
I'm not feeling
very well. I have
to go home," she said, hurrying to the
front door.

"Mia, wait! I'll call your grandmother,"
Emily's mom said worriedly.

"It's okay, I'll be fine," Mia called
back, tears already stinging her eyes as
she wrestled with the front door lock.
At last it opened, and she dashed down
the front walk.

Meowing frantically, Whiskers made a flying leap off of Emily's knee and chased after her. Where was she going? She hadn't even tickled his ears and scratched under his chin, like she usually did when she left.

He shot out the front door, onto the path, and looked around. He'd never been out in the front of the house—only on carefully guarded trips into the backyard. The grass was frozen over with a layer of frost, and snowflakes were flurrying down from the darkening sky. If Mia had been with him, Whiskers would have chased the strange fluffy things, but now he hardly noticed them. He had no idea where Mia had gone. He sat down on the path and wailed for her.

But Mia couldn't hear him. She

was almost home now, and she could hardly see through her tears, let alone hear a heartbroken kitten halfway up the road. She pressed the front doorbell over and over till Gran came, looking worried.

"Oh, it's you, Mia! But I was coming to get you . . . Mia, what's wrong?"

"Whiskers," Mia sobbed. "I was too late for Whiskers. I should have said I loved him, and I didn't. How could

I be so stupid? You were right all along, Gran, and now I've lost him!"

Gran hugged her. "Oh, Mia. I'm so sorry. Has someone taken him?"

Mia nodded. "A lady's coming to see him tomorrow, and she's going to love him, I know she will."

"Tomorrow?" Gran drew her inside and shut the door. "But Mia, why don't you go back to Emily and her mom and explain? Tell them you want him."

"But I can't!" Mia wailed. "I kept saying no, because of Sandy. They'll think I'm just going to change my mind again. And I told Dad that I never ever wanted another cat. Dad and Mom would never let me have Whiskers now." She sat down on the bottom step with her face in her hands.

"Miriam—the lady who called—she knows all about nervous cats, and she really wants him. Whiskers deserves to have an owner like that." She sniffed. "I should have been braver before."

Gran sat down next to her, rather carefully. "I do see what you mean, Mia, but I think you're being too hard on yourself—and that poor little cat." She stared thoughtfully at the front door, and a small smile curved up the corners of her mouth.

Mia didn't see it—she had her fingers pressed against her eyes now, to stop herself from crying. She could see white speckles against her eyelids, and they reminded her of kitten fur.

"Are you sure?" Emily wrinkled her nose anxiously and glanced up, checking that Mrs. Jones hadn't seen them talking. "Won't it just make you feel worse?"

Mia shook her head. "No. I really want to say good-bye to him. I have to. I probably will feel horrible, but it would be awful to never see him again."

"I guess you're right." Emily sighed. "Miriam sounded really nice, from what Mom said."

"I know," Mia whispered. Then she shook her head, trying not to think about saying good-bye to Whiskers. "We're supposed to be writing about Victorian animals. Did you bring that book from the library?"

They kept working—Mrs. Jones had said their project idea sounded excellent. But every time she stopped writing, Mia felt sad again, remembering Whiskers's soft white fur and those amazing whiskers! He was so different from Sandy, but he was special, too. The way he always wanted to climb all over her, and the funny way he perched on her shoulder.

He'll be too big to do that soon, though, she thought. She'd never see what he looked like as a grown-up cat! Mia swallowed miserably.

She wasn't sure if the day raced by, or if it crawled. All their classes seemed to last forever, but the end of the school day came so quickly. It seemed that all of a sudden she was putting on her coat, grabbing her stuff, and following Emily to meet Emily's mom outside the gates. And the walk home seemed to vanish in seconds. Mia felt almost sick as they went into Emily's house.

She expected Whiskers to bounce up to her, purring, as he usually did, but the house was very quiet—Silky and Satin were curled up together in Silky's old basket.

Mia swallowed. "Where's Whiskers?" she asked Emily's mom.

She looked around, hoping that he was hiding, and he was going to jump out and surprise her. But really, she knew that he wasn't. "He's gone, isn't he? That lady's already come and taken him?"

Emily's mom was starting to say something, but Mia couldn't bear to listen. She was too late—even to say good-bye!

Emily rushed over and tried to give her a hug, but Mia gently pushed her away and ran home.

Gran answered the door, looking excited, but Mia hardly saw her. She didn't even stop to listen to what Gran was trying to say. She simply raced up the stairs to the safety of her bedroom, flinging herself onto her bed and hugging Sandy's old blanket.

Now she had lost both of them.

Chapter Eight

Whiskers sniffed around the strange room worriedly. He didn't understand what was going on. He had been carried here in a box, and he hadn't liked it—his claws caught and scratched on the cardboard as he slid around, meowing and hissing. Then he'd been let out in this strange new place. He was sure he'd never been here before, but it smelled familiar somehow, and there was a bowl of his favorite food, and some water. The old lady had watched him, but she hadn't tried to pick him up. She'd just sat, very quietly, and every so often she murmured gently to him. He knew her. She came to visit with Mia sometimes—so why was she here, when Mia wasn't?

It was all very odd. He'd hoped that Mia might come and see him, after she disappeared so quickly the day before. But what if she didn't know where he was? He needed to get back home so Mia could find him.

The old lady had gone away now. She had hurried off when that doorbell rang. She'd closed the door behind her, Whiskers noticed as he sniffed at it.

Or almost, anyway. The latch hadn't quite caught. Whiskers nosed the door, and it swung open a little more. The curious kitten poked his whiskers around the door, and then his nose, and then the rest of him, and he set off to search for Mia.

Whiskers pattered down the hallway, his nose twitching. He felt confused. Maybe Mia had come to find him after all. He was sure he could smell her. Or was he imagining it? He looked from side to side, wondering where to go. Food smells were coming from behind him, but from the noise it sounded like there were people upstairs. Stairs . . .

He trotted over and looked up the flight of stairs. They were very steep.

Luckily, they had carpet, or he would never have been able to get his claws in to struggle up. Whiskers scrambled up onto the first step, feeling proud of himself. He licked his paw and brushed it over his ears to settle his fur before he tackled the next step. And the next . . .

It took him a good few minutes to heave and claw his way up to the landing, and he rolled onto the last step, panting exhaustedly. His claws ached. But he was up! And he could hear voices coming from behind a door at the top of the stairs. His ears flattened back. They were not good voices. Someone was upset. The second voice was the old lady who had been with him downstairs. She was doing that gentle, soothing talking again.

The door was open a crack, and he peered cautiously around it. The old lady was sitting on the bed with a girl lying facedown beside her, patting her hair while she cried. Whiskers sniffed again. He'd never heard Mia sound like that before, but he was sure it was Mia. Would she be glad to see him? What was the matter with her? He hesitated by the door, uncertain about what to do.

Then the old lady looked up and saw him. She looked surprised for a moment, but then she smiled and held out her hand to him, rubbing her fingers together, her face hopeful.

She wanted him to come closer.

"Mia, sweetheart, listen. I've got something to tell you. I'd have told you right away, if it hadn't taken me so long to get up those stairs."

"Sorry, Gran. I know you're not supposed to use the stairs. Oh, I should have told Emily's mom a long time ago that I wanted Whiskers to be ours . . ." a muffled voice sobbed.

That was his name. It *was* Mia—it had to be. She smelled right, and she'd said his name, even if her voice sounded all strange.

Whiskers bounded across the bedroom and looked up at the bed with frustration. How was he supposed to get up there? The old lady stretched out her hand and scooped him up, smiling. "Mia . . ."

He had been right! Whiskers stumbled along the soft comforter until he was standing on a dark fleecy blanket next to Mia's tangle of fair hair. He nudged her with his nose, but she didn't notice, so he did it again, harder this time.

Mia raised her head. Her eyes were blurry and sore from crying, so for a moment she didn't understand.

Then Whiskers purred at her proudly. He had found her!

"Whiskers!" Mia gasped. "What are you doing here? Why aren't you at your new home? Did you run away? Emily's going to be so worried about you." She struggled to sit up, and gazed at the little white kitten sitting contentedly in the middle of her bed.

"That's what I was trying to tell you," Gran said gently. "When you came home so upset last night, I had a talk with your mom and dad, and we all agreed. Your dad had been convinced that you should have Whiskers anyway. He wanted to bring him home a long time ago, but your mom was worried it would upset you again. So Dad and I went over to Emily's house and talked to her mom after you'd gone off to school this morning. We arranged for Whiskers to be your kitten. Well, and a little bit mine, for some company while you're at school. I know you shouldn't give animals as presents, but think of him as an early Christmas gift." Gran smiled at her, a little anxiously. "Your mom was so upset that she had to be at work this afternoon. She wanted to see your face when you found out."

"But what about the lady who called? Miriam?" Mia murmured. Her mind was whirring, trying to take all this in.

"Emily's mom called her to explain. She was very sympathetic, apparently.

She lost a cat recently, too. She said she knew how hard it could be."

"So Whiskers is really ours?" Mia looked down at the kitten, who was sniffing the cat blanket interestedly, his whiskers looking remarkably white against the navy-blue fleece. She reached out and tickled him under the chin with just one finger. She didn't dare do more. She felt like there was a dream kitten in her bedroom and if she touched him, he might disappear, like a bubble.

But he didn't. He purred loudly and gazed up at her with big blue eyes. He looked very, very pleased with himself.

"Yes, you are a smart little cat, finding your way up here," Gran said, smiling. "I thought I'd shut him in my living room, Mia, since I didn't want him wandering all over the house, feeling lost. But he obviously found a way out. He wanted to come and find you."

Mia nodded. "He's sitting on Sandy's blanket," she whispered suddenly, a strange sharp feeling clutching at her chest.

Gran nodded. "Yes."

Mia took a deep breath. Whiskers nudged her knee with his nose and stood up, turning around a couple of times before settling himself into the perfect position, nose touching tail tip, like a little white fur cushion.

Mia let the breath out again, shakily. There were white hairs on the blanket now, mixed with the orange ones.

Whiskers opened one eye and yawned, showing a raspberry-pink tongue. Then he snuggled down deeper into the blanket and went to sleep.

Just like he belonged.

Mia yawned and rolled over, and felt Whiskers sigh in his sleep beside her. She'd had to move the fleece blanket now, to the side of her bed. Whiskers liked to sleep jammed between her and the wall, even though Mia sometimes worried that she would accidentally squish him.

She buried her head in her pillow and sighed happily. It didn't feel like time to get up yet. Then her eyes snapped open. It was Christmas Day!

"Whiskers! Look—my Christmas stocking." She sat up and eyed the bulging red-and-white-striped stocking happily. She could see a packet of her favorite candy sticking out of it. "And cat treats, look! Your favorite fishy ones!"

Whiskers purred with pleasure. He didn't know why Mia wanted to wake up early, but he would do anything for fishy treats. He batted happily at the ribbons as Mia unwrapped her stocking presents.

"It's nearly seven o'clock," Mia said at last. "I wonder if Mom and Dad

would mind being woken up yet? Or Gran?"

She climbed out of bed, shrugged on her robe, then padded out onto the landing, with Whiskers following her. She peeped in her mom and dad's bedroom door, but they were both still fast asleep. Dad had said last night that his best Christmas present would be to sleep in, so she scooped Whiskers up before he could go and leap onto the bed. He'd only been with them a week, but already he had a thing about Dad's feet. He liked to pounce on them, and Mia thought that probably wouldn't be Dad's ideal way to wake up.

She crept down the stairs. Gran always woke up early. She said it had to do with being over seventy—she didn't need as much sleep anymore.

"I can hear you, Mia! Merry Christmas!" Gran called as Mia hesitated outside her door.

Mia slipped into Gran's little apartment. "You're up already!" she said in surprise. Gran was sitting in her armchair, with a magazine and a cup of tea.

"Yes, and I'm glad you're here. I've got a special present for you." Gran reached over to her little table and picked up a flat, rectangular package, wrapped in shiny Christmas paper with a big bow. Gran liked wrapping presents.

"'For Mia, with lots of love this Christmas—and for being brave,'" Mia read from the gift tag. "I don't understand."

"Open it, Mia, and you'll see." Gran nodded eagerly.

Mia put Whiskers down on the floor, then started to undo the bow and peel off the paper.

"Oh, Gran! It's great!" It looked like

a box, with a beautiful painting of a cat on the lid.

"Ah, you haven't seen inside it yet—open it up."

It wasn't actually a box, Mia realized as she opened it. It was a hinged photo frame, made to hold two photos, one beside the other.

As though it was made for pictures of two very special cats.

Mia smiled, her eyes blurring a little with tears, but only happy ones. On the left was Sandy, staring out at her, with his ears pricked up. Gran must have taken it just as he spotted a butterfly to chase, Mia thought. Sandy had loved to hunt butterflies.

And on the right was a picture of her little Whiskers, sitting on Gran's windowsill. The winter sun was shining on his magnificent whiskers so that they sparkled.

"Thanks, Gran, it's the best present." Mia hugged her, and laughed as there was a sudden rustling sound. Whiskers had jumped onto the discarded wrapping paper and was pouncing backward and forward, chasing something imaginary. Maybe when he was bigger, Whiskers would chase butterflies, too. . . .

Also Available:

Lost in the Snow
Holly Webb
SCHOLASTIC

Lost in the Storm
Holly Webb
SCHOLASTIC

Sky the Unwanted Kitten
Holly Webb
SCHOLASTIC

Ginger the Stray Kitten
Holly Webb
SCHOLASTIC

Harry the Homeless Puppy
Holly Webb
SCHOLASTIC

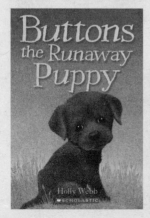

Buttons the Runaway Puppy
Holly Webb
SCHOLASTIC

Oscar's Lonely Christmas
Holly Webb
SCHOLASTIC

Alone in the Night
Holly Webb
SCHOLASTIC

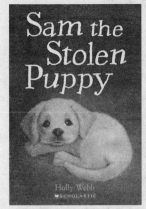

Sam the Stolen Puppy

Holly Webb
SCHOLASTIC

Alfie all Alone

Holly Webb
SCHOLASTIC

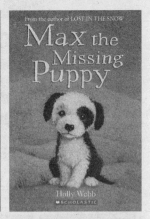

From the author of LOST IN THE SNOW

Max the Missing Puppy

Holly Webb
SCHOLASTIC

Timmy in Trouble

Holly Webb
SCHOLASTIC

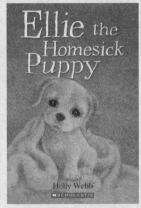

Ellie the Homesick Puppy

Holly Webb
SCHOLASTIC

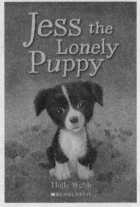

Jess the Lonely Puppy

Holly Webb
SCHOLASTIC

Misty the Abandoned Kitten

Holly Webb
SCHOLASTIC

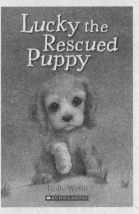

Lucky the Rescued Puppy

Holly Webb
SCHOLASTIC

THE PUPPY PLACE

SO MANY PERFECT PUPPIES - COLLECT THEM ALL!

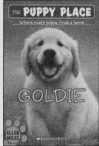 GOLDIE

 SNOWBALL

 SHADOW

 RASCAL

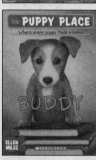 BUDDY

 FLASH

 SCOUT

 PATCHES

 PUGSLEY

 MAGGIE and MAX

 NOODLE

 PRINCESS

 CODY

 BEAR

 HONEY

 LUCKY

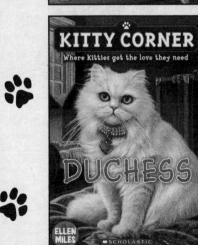
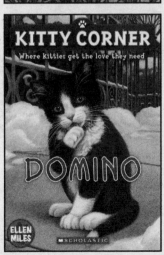

My Naughty Little Puppy

Holly Webb

When Ellie names her puppy Rascal, she doesn't
realize how right she is! The playful little puppy is soon
getting himself and Ellie into all sorts of mischief. . . .

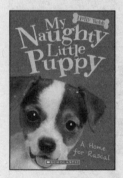  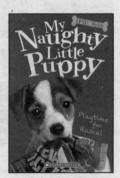